PASSAGE THROUGH TIME

"A Scottish Historical Time Travel Romance"

William Newell

© 2015 SubArctic Publishing

Disclaimer

Stories In This Series:

Book One: Passage Through Time

Book Two: Return to Scotland

Book Three: The Forbidden Rescue

Book Four: Alone in Time

Book Five: One Last Time

Dedication

"To all who long to live the romantic era.

This book was created for you."

CONTENTS

Chapter 1

A Long Vacation

Edinburgh, Scotland

June 14, 2015

"If we leave at nine, we should be in Glasgow by ten." John Duncan announced after staring for a long time at his smart phone. He stroked his short-clipped, brown beard as he considered the directions. "That would give us plenty of time for check-in, I'd imagine."

He and his wife were standing in front of their Queen Street, Edinburgh hotel on a sunny, summer day. Both were drenched in sweat and slightly winded from having hiked Holyrood.

"Yeah, that's just great." Katie snapped. Her knees ached and her back was sore. "I wouldn't want to slow down the whole Scottish vacation experience by, you know, actually experiencing any of it."

"What's that supposed to mean?" John jammed his phone into his shorts pocket, barely making eye contact with his wife.

She folded her arms and glared at her husband. "Oh, I don't know. Let's see. We walk by parliament and you tell me the entire history of the building. We hike Holyrood and I'm getting a history lesson not only of Edinburgh in one ear, but of Scottish independence, Picts, the Clearances- I try to enjoy our picnic, and you start in on me with how brie is made."

"Someone has to say something." He grumbled as they entered their hotel lobby. "Maybe if you contributed to a conversation once in a while instead of complaining about everything-"

"I contribute plenty! Is it my fault you never listen to me?"

The American tourists carried on their irritated bickering into the elevator, up to the fourth floor, and right up to the door of their suite. As John fumbled for the keys, Katie stopped him by putting her hand on his. "Look. I'm tired. It's been a long day already. I just need a little… quiet, and a shower and maybe a nap. Okay?"

"Yeah." He sounded tense, not ready to be conciliatory. He opened the door and immediately dropped into the couch, assuming a subdued, quieter attitude. "Shower is yours."

If he wasn't arguing, it was a step towards peace, Katie knew, so she allowed the moment to lapse without comment. "Thanks," she replied, heading for their room and bath.

After washing up, she spread out on the bed wearing nothing but panties and a t-shirt. The sun was surprisingly bright for a country known for its clouds and rain, and it poured through her window and onto the bed, warming and drying her. She rolled over and looked away from the light, listening as John vegged out on British T.V.

She had hoped the trip would change things. It hadn't. They were still arguing, disconnected from each other. They seemed to have brought their emotional baggage with them from Chicago.

Back home, she'd been quick to lose patience with John. He'd grown more obsessed with his hobbies- photography, history, music- and had neglected her whenever she wanted a night with just the two of them. Meanwhile, her long hours as a struggling reporter hadn't helped matters.

And to make matters worse, she'd be thirty in a week. Thirty. It hadn't been a big deal to John two years ago when he'd left his twenties behind; they'd gone on a road trip with their friends June and Bobby Shoenfeld down to Mammoth Caves, Kentucky and had had a blast together. Of course, then June had gotten pregnant, and they were seeing less and less of their friends.

If she fell asleep on the bed with her long, red hair wet, she'd be sorry. Instead, she hopped up and got out the blow dryer.

John hollered something from the front room she couldn't hear, so she flipped the switch. "What?"

"I said, do you have to do that right now?" John shouted from the front room.

She gripped the handle of the dryer, counting to ten. When she'd calmed, she opened the door and explained, "I need to, yes, or it'll be a mess. Okay?"

"Sure." He glanced over at her from the couch and then did a double-take. "Wow."

"What?" She self-consciously played with her hair.

"You look... well, you look sexy." His smile and interest was genuine.

She hadn't been expecting that and wasn't sure how to react. "It's just a t-shirt." She found herself shyly smiling at the compliment.

"You wear it well. And, you know, no pants, wet hair. Kind of a turn-on, babe."

She leaned against the doorway slightly. "I see. You sound like a man who wants to apologize for being so snippy with his wife."

He turned off the TV, got up, and crossed the room to her. "His beautiful wife." He slipped his hands around her waist and she relaxed into his embrace. "I'm going to grab a quick shower."

"I kind of like you sweaty." She said quietly, but then noticed an unpleasant, earthy smell about him. "Well- okay, maybe not sweaty and grubby." She laughed.

He chuckled and went to the bathroom. "Don't start without me!" He teased. She threw a pillow at him.

Back on the bed, curled up and listening to the shower run, she sighed. They were so volatile and mood swingy. Was it her? She didn't think it was just her. He was quicker to lose his patience, or so it seemed to her. The sex was still good; at least that part of their relationship was working. But it couldn't paper over the terrible news that had set their lives on edge. She started to cry, thinking about that day, then brushed the tears away.

She was finally due some happiness. Their first week in Scotland had been less than amazing. Edinburgh was a pretty town with a lot to see and do, but she wanted to see Glasgow very badly. Her grandparents had come to America from Glasgow; the Cathcarts had deep roots in the town going back centuries.

The light was shining in her eyes, so she got up and closed the windows. They were heavy curtains, helping to plunge the room into a thick semi-dark. She lay back down. He was kind of taking his time. Didn't he want to be with her? She laughed at herself. Of course, he was just that dirty. It'd take some time.

The bed felt extremely comfy as she snuggled in. Maybe it'd be okay if she rested her eyes.

It was extremely dark outside, she found, when John shook her awake. "Time to get up. We've got a train to catch."

She heard the note of disappointment in his voice and frowned. It would be a very long train ride, indeed.

~ Passage Through Time ~

Chapter 2

The Book

Glasgow, Scotland

June 15, 2015

Katie hadn't been all that interested in history prior to arriving in Glasgow. But after the long, almost silent train trip across the narrow central valley of Scotland, she'd begun to feel like she needed to work harder to connect with her increasingly distant husband.

"You're sure you don't mind?" It felt like the third time he'd asked this morning. She stowed away her annoyance.

"Of course not! I'm excited about seeing medieval... stuff." She trailed off.

He cracked up at this as they walked. "Stuff. Right."

"No, seriously! Swords and armor and wizards. They get me hot."

"Uh huh."

"Hogwarts is around here somewhere, right?" She asked, keeping a straight face.

"Okay." He tried to tickle her as she stepped out his reach.

"Seriously," she carried on as they came within view of the museum. "If we have time to dig up anything on my family, that'd be nice."

"I thought your family was Swedish?" He asked, a confused look passing over his face.

She stopped putting her hands on her hips. "My Dad's, yeah. My Mom's family is Scottish, thank you very much, and they're from Glasgow. There's a town named Cathcart near here too. Like my maiden name?"

"Oh." He looked embarrassed as he tugged his tweed duffer cap down. He was looking a little more hipster than usual, between the cap, beard, and a grey vest over his white t-shirt. She missed the days when he'd been a musician and she'd been in the audience, cheering him on. He still made music, but there were no shows and no band. It was all done on computers and in his study, a place she'd come to loathe. Whenever he closed the door of that room, he was shutting her out.

"It's okay." She dismissed the issue, not wanting anything to potentially come between them today. She had woken up determined they'd get through the day without a single fight or unkind word.

"Well, Duncans are from Glasgow as well." He noted. "Not all of them, of course. But most of my ancestors grew up here."

"I didn't know that! I thought they were from Edinburgh."

"Nope, Glasgow. I told you that." He sounded annoyed for a second, then laughed it off. "I guess neither of us is listening to the other very well lately."

"We're not. Try to do better?"

"You bet, Katie." He kissed her forehead.

They paid for their tickets and when they were in the museum, Katie had to admit to herself that she was impressed by the displays. Yes, there were suits of armor and swords, of course, and John was instantly drawn to those images of martial warriors reflected in the past. While Katie checked these out to be polite, she was far more drawn to the colorful tapestries on the wall. She could almost see the bright reds and blues that had since faded, the images of unicorns, ladies, and wild creatures wandering in forests and fields. It was a fascinating look at what the world must have seemed like to people of that time, and far more attractive to her than implements of death.

As she wandered the museum- now separated from John, who was busy reading the description of a two-handed sword- Katie couldn't help but notice that a strange little man was following her. She didn't feel threatened; she doubted the grey-haired man, with his owl-like glasses and goatee had ever seemed threatening to anyone in his entire life. However, she wasn't enjoying being stared at, so she whirled on him as he was peeking at her from over a guidebook.

"Can I help you?" She asked abruptly. He jumped from behind the little book and his glasses went a touch askew. He reached up and set them right.

"I- I- oh, dear, do forgive me." The man had an English accent, which didn't surprise her at all. She guessed he had to be an academic and he instantly confirmed her suspicion. "I am Dr. Oscar Wellesley." He extended a hand, and the way in which he said his name, she sounded as though he expected to be recognized.

"Katie Duncan." She shook his hand. "Have we met?"

He looked perturbed that she'd never heard his name. "Well. No, not exactly. You're an American, I see. I thought you must be from Glasgow and- well, I won't trouble you."

"It's fine."

There was a question on his mind, and he found the courage to ask. "You wouldn't happen to have ancestors from this part of the country?"

She sighed. What did he want? John walked over just then. "My husband, John. John, Dr. Oscar Wellesley" She introduced the men. He started just as suddenly at the sight of her man as he had when he'd met Katie.

"I'm - please forgive me, this is a bit of a shock." Dr. Wellesley proclaimed, dabbing at his forehead. "I hardly expected to see two people who so closely resembled... well, the coincidence is astonishing. You even have his beard!"

John gave the short man an amused smirk. "Let me guess. I look just like William Wallace, right? Freedom!" He pretended to hold up a sword, and Katie snickered at the gesture. He was a dork, but she preferred him that way.

The professor was far less amused. "I can see why you might think it's a laughing matter, naturally. It's not. I think if you could see their images, you'd understand."

Surprising them both, Wellesley gave a short, barking little laugh. "What am I saying? Of course you can see them. The museum has a private library in the basement. Would you care to see what I'm talking about? I have a pass, so it's completely fine." He held up a card that appeared to be an electronic key card.

John looked to Katie. She shrugged. "Why not? I don't suppose everyone gets to see the museum's private library. John?"

"I'm game!"

"Very good." He led them to the back of the building to a heavy-looking door with a sign on it, "Not Open to the Public." He gave them access with a quick pass of his card over a reader beside the door. When the reader beeped green, he quickly opened the door and they followed him down a brief flight of stairs.

Below the museum there was a library; untidy and cluttered, it was more of a collection of old books stacked haphazardly on shelves. However, Professor Wellesley knew exactly what he was looking for and was making a beeline through the shelves to his destination. Partway down an aisle, he pointed back to the main aisle they'd come from. "Follow that to the end and you'll see a table. Have a seat; I'll bring the book to you."

"Fine." John said for them both, and they found their way as directed to a thick, dark-wood table. There was a metal lamp stuck in the middle of the table, offering a glum amount of light. The overhead lights weren't very good, mostly flickering and in desperate need of changing. Much of the library had become heavily cloaked in spider webs, dust, and a musty odor.

When they sat, John gave her an amused smile and did a short circle with his finger around his ear.

"Behave." Katie whispered. "He's harmless."

"Here it is!" The Professor called out. She motioned for John to be still, and he listened to her, putting on a fake, interested smile as the older man met them at their table.

"Very old" John noted, and they both saw that Wellesley was wearing gloves. "Good idea."

"Hmm? Yes, essential really. Now, this book is quite the rarity for two reasons. Firstly, it's not a Bible. Secondly, it dates to 1685 making it one of the oldest non-Bibles in Scotland and the oldest in this collection. I must caution you to only permit me to touch the pages, do you understand?"

"Sure." John replied.

The book was carefully opened and laid out before them. With amazing care, Wellesley turned the pages until he'd reached a full-page illustration. The Duncans looked and each felt a range of wild emotions.

They were looking at two ancient warriors. Despite one being female, she was clearly a fighter and, standing in front of the male, appeared to be the superior officer between them. Despite the years and Roman-era painting style, John and Katie were clearly looking at reflections of their own faces.

"Now, we don't know the source of this illustration, but it certainly is much older than the book," Wellesley was saying, but to Katie his voice sounded very far away. This woman could have been her most ancient ancestor. The artistry, while somewhat fanciful in creating the background, gave incredible detail to her smallish nose, her wild, flowing red hair, her high cheekbones.

"This- wow. So how old is the illustration?" John asked, stunned to seriousness.

"We honestly don't know. It's impossible to say. We believe these to be Pictish warriors, so named by their biographers, not themselves. We have almost none of their writing. If this illustration were created by a Pictish artist, it would be one of the earliest non-carved Pictish illustrations known to us; but I expect a Roman did this work. Ancient Scots weren't known for creating lifelike, realistic depictions of people with paint as the Romans did. They were much more likely to carve than paint, and their carvings are truly remarkable. Then again, they may have created books and artwork, not unlike the Book of Kells in Ireland. We simply don't know yet.

He paused to rub the bridge of his nose before replacing his glasses. "The Picts are something of a lost people to us. Or- they could even be Caledonians. Much earlier than the Picts. I suspect not, but we can't be sure."

John started to read the opposite page. "There's a story here, and if I'm reading this right it's about these two people. Have you read it?"

"Not this part of the book as of yet, no." Wellesley explained, apologetically. "I'll tell you what. Let me get a second book, a reference book, and I'll be right back. I'll read some of this to you, shall I? I realize the script may be difficult to decipher."

They agreed and he disappeared among the books. "What do you think?" John asked Katie. By his wide-eyes, he was clearly freaked out and excited by what he was seeing. Even so, he gave a huge yawn.

"It's incredible. This woman could be my twin." Katie tried to say. As she voiced the word twin, she gave a mighty yawn of her own. She suddenly felt an overwhelming sense of exhaustion. She sat back in her chair, and as she did so, felt she was falling. John was also dropping his head onto the table. The dim lights around them popped out, one by one in rapid succession, until the lamp on the table was their only light, growing dimmer and dimmer.

"What the hell." She barely managed to say as the chair back melted behind her. There was no stone floor to greet her, no impact. Just darkness.

~ Passage Through Time ~

Chapter 3

Chaos

Near the Antonine Wall, Tribal Lands, Caledonia

Summer, 210 AD

"Defend her!"

Katie was laying on the ground, or more properly, face-down in the mud. She lifted herself up from the mixture of grime and broken grass and what she saw instantly terrified her.

There were bare legs pumping, feet flying, and bodies strewn across a muddy field before her. The people she saw were mostly in front of her view. She felt strong arms lifting her up.

"Your warrior maidens are with you! Those who breathe." A woman shouted into her ears. The language was strange. Why did she understand it? It seemed both foreign and familiar. It was definitely not English, yet she was able to understand every word as though it were her native tongue.

As she was lifted to her feet, she found that both hands were holding something heavy and wooden. It was an axe, its metal head drenched in blood. She shifted it to one hand and found it was actually meant to be a single-handed weapon. Instinctively, it felt right in her hand.

It was strange that it should feel that way. How was it even possible? Everything she saw resembled a battle re-enactment. However, re-enactors didn't usually lose their limbs and heads, as she was seeing ahead in the nearby skirmish.

On the ground beside her, she spied a strange, oval thing; she bent and snatched it up. This was her shield. Katie had no idea why she knew this.

"Kate!" One of the women who had lifted her was shouting in her ear. "They are coming again! We must melt away into the woods, while we still can!"

She looked about her. She didn't understand what she was seeing. There was blood, an astonishing amount of it sprayed across the landscape. Horrifically, there were bodies and far too many body parts as well. She felt tears well up and covered her mouth with her hand, wanting to look away.

"Are you wounded?" Her friend was shouting at her. The woman was dark-haired and hugely-muscled. There were virtually no other women on the field, other than the six or so surrounding her. One woman lay nearby, clearly dead. A sense of sadness overtook her as she saw the girl must have been only a teen. If this were a war game, it was brutal and grotesque.

Her gaze wandered and she spied a soldier- she now presumed them to be Celts of some sort, not entirely sure what she was seeing - and the man had a spear tip buried into his foot. He had fallen and was clutching the wound, grimacing. He turned his head and she felt yet another wave of shock atop all the strangeness of the past few minutes.

"Katie?" He called out, his voice filled with pain.

"John! Dear God!" She tried to push her way toward him, but the women held her back.

"Cousin, are you hurt? Tell me first." Her protecting dark-haired woman warrior asked.

"We have to go to him!" She shouted in the woman's face. Surrendering further effort to restrain her, the women moved forward and in a moment, had surrounded John.

"We've gone to him, as you said, sister. Now give us your orders, Kate, or we are lost!" Her ally shouted in her face. She felt overwhelmed.

She threw down her sword and shield and helped prop John up. Her women bodyguards were shocked by her behavior, but one of them quickly snapped up her gear from the ground.

"Retreat! Into the woods!" Katie shouted in a quavering voice. Another woman helped her with John, who limped as fast as he could between them.

The woods was fortunately nearby. She and the Celts- were they Celts? She wasn't sure what they were- rushed into the cover of the trees. For some reason, whatever the force was that they were fighting had apparently decided to allow them to their tactical retreat.

They ran as fast as they were able. With John's wounds slowing them, Katie and her group fell further behind the others. Yet soon enough they were deep in the dark, shady forest. Her fighters were returning to her, in apparently good spirits.

"A good raid, Kate!" A man yelled out and clapped her on the back. He looked with some disgust at John. "Why have you spared any strength for this worthless one, Kate? He has merely stubbed his toe!" He pointed to the foot wound and laughed. He was joined by nearby fighters, including Katie's bodyguards.

"Enough!" She shouted out. Though Katie was shaking and afraid, she recognized that she was viewed as being in charge of whomever these people were. She suspected her behavior would help to determine how John was treated. "He is wounded, yes. But I also saw this man fight to defend me and to protect all of us. He was both noble and brave!"

None of this was true. She hadn't seen anything prior to waking up in the mud. But she supposed a statement of his military credibility was called for.

"It's true." Her friend the dark-haired woman declared. "I saw him as well. He killed several of the African invaders."

Africans? That was a weird statement. She hadn't seen the enemy clearly, though they wore strange armor, like Roman soldiers. She nodded all the same.

There was some grumbling and discussion among the warriors, but they seemed to buy her story. The man who'd clapped her on the back walked over to John and gave him his own backslap. "Your bravery is an inspiration to us all, Nechtan."

"I wouldn't have survived without my kin." John replied, keeping a steady voice. But Katie knew him well enough that she could see her husband was rattled by being called such a strange name. Worse, he was in horrendous pain.

"We return now to the village. Move!" The other man shouted. He looked back to Katie, apparently double-checking that she agreed. She gave a nod.

As they marched, now following a well-worn path in the heart of the forest, she continued to help John with his hobbling journey. She whispered into his ear. "What the hell is this?"

"Roman-era Scotland." He breathed into her ear. "Before the Picts, even. Caledonians."

"Jesus."

"Yeah, he wasn't born that long ago." John joked.

"You think this is funny?"

"No, but if you'll excuse me Queen Katie, I was just stabbed in the foot. Do you mind if I crack a joke or two?"

"No. I... I guess you're certainly entitled."

"Thank you, your majesty." He gave a little bow, and she tried to stifle a laugh.

"What do we do?"

"Do what I'm doing. Play along, for now." He suggested.

That might be easier said than done, she thought, especially since she couldn't understand how they had found themselves in a situation where playing along might decide whether they lived or died.

Chapter 4

In the Village of Loxa

Village of Loxa, Caledonia

Summer, 210 AD

"He'll likely recover, in time." The village healer told Katie after she'd fully bandaged John. A serious-minded old woman with hair as white as fingernail ends, she had spent a great deal of time treating and bandaging John's mangled foot.

"You're sure?" Katie asked. She was standing outside of the hide-covered tent where he was being treated. She presumed it was his home. She wasn't sure where she lived yet, but that would be something she'd figure out in time. All she knew was that the little village surrounded by a wooden palisade was called Loxa.

"Your warrior has suffered a serious injury whatever the others may say. He is strong and will be fine. But he should rest now."

"I'd like to speak with him first."

The woman seemed reluctant. "It would be best if he were left alone. But if you wish to see him, I won't stand in your way."

"I do." She insisted.

"Very well." The woman was apparently used to Katie having her way. She gave her a smile of thanks and entered the tent.

John had been wearing a tunic and checked pants, now discarded and lying beside his bed. He was covered in a simple sheet, wearing only silver bracelets and a silver, ornate half-circle. She, too had a number of pieces of jewelry that decorated her, including brooches, pins, and rings.

"John." She knelt beside him and took his hand. He was sweating and looked tired. "How do you feel, babe?"

"Been better." He nodded. "Not every day you get to go back in time and immediately take a spear to the foot. You know... we guys fantasize about this stuff. We do! And I have to say I'm pretty unimpressed with my performance. I mean, I didn't even get to lop the head off a Roman soldier."

She chuckled. "You're going to be okay according to the old woman."

"Fyfa? She's a smart one. Seems to know all about our history and past, if you want to refresh your memory on our apparent years of growing up here which we both conveniently no longer recall. Also, she can tell we're, uh, different."

"How so?" She felt a twinge of alarm. That could be dangerous.

"She kept mumbling that we had both been to the other side. Didn't seem very upset by it. She's a mystical woman, whatever else she is. I think you can rely on her."

"Good." She thought carefully before speaking, keeping her voice low. She didn't want anyone to overhear their conversation, as it could cause trouble if people suspected they weren't entirely who they claimed to be. "By any chance did you get any other names? So I can pretend I know people? No one has used their names really since we came back. I'm surprised to hear I'm Kate."

"Yes, but they pronounce it a little different. Did you notice that? Anyway, your buddy, the woman who behaves like your second-in-command? She's your sister Beitidh. The man who approached us in the woods is called Caltram. He's one of the war leaders. I'm going to go out on a limb and say that you were- sorry, this may come as a bit of a shock- married, and that you have inherited leadership of the tribe after your hubby died in battle. You became leader on the say so of Caltram and Beitidh. Oh- and they're an item. Not officially, I guess."

"You got all that from the healer while she was mending you?" Her eyes went wide with surprise. "I'm impressed. You have an ear for gossip."

"She's chatty. Doesn't hurt that I'm so handsome." He pretended to primp his beard.

She bent down and kissed him. He reached up from his bed to run his hands through her hair, gently caressing her. When she came up for a breath, he sighed. "More handsome than I guessed." He teased.

"No, still a frog and not a prince. I'm just used to your face." She assured him.

"Have it your way, love."

"I will. How are we going to get out of this? How do we get back to our time?" Her voice nearly broke as she spoke, but he wiped away the beginning of a tear.

"Not now. We'll figure it out later."

"Right. Okay. I'd better get home, wherever that is. Be careful, dear."

"I intend to."

She left his tent and found Beitidh standing outside, her arms folded defensively. Her thick eyebrows expressed worry. "Kate. May I have a word?"

"Of course, sister. Why don't we walk to my home?" She chose her words carefully. It had occurred to her that if she let Beitidh slightly lead them, they might find the location without giving away her ignorance.

The other woman walked beside her, looking uncomfortable. "I wish to speak to you of Nechtan."

"Go on."

"You know as well as I that he was running away from the skirmish when the Africans met the battle." She sounded very disapproving. "You should have left him to his fate."

"I know." Contradicting her seemed like it wouldn't be productive or helpful, so she opted to improvise. Everything had become improvisation of late. It was a necessary survival skill, when trapped in a bizarre situation, she decided. "I see something in him, though. I believe he can do better in the future. A second chance could be the making of the man."

Beitidh looked doubtful. "I would never question your decisions. You know this. But does it set a good example for Lair to save such a weak-willed man from a much deserved fate? You will teach him weakness when he must demonstrate strength. And besides, there are men who covet your position in the clan."

Ignoring the strange name, she decided to take a different approach. "If I don't object to Caltram, you should say nothing about Nechtan."

"Aha!" The tall woman gave her a hearty push, nearly causing her to stumble. "I knew it! If you were taking Nechtan to your bed, why didn't you just say so? You've been holding back, sister!"

They had reached a small hut where Beitidh gave her a brief, warm hug. "You really must give me some notion as to the men you pursue in the future. I was ready to offer the fool up for sacrifice then and there! Let me know your mind."

"I will sister."

She stepped into her little hut, ready to sleep, not even hungry or wishing anything but sleep. Instead, she was surprised to see a young girl cooking over a fire in the center of the room. The girl looked up and smiled as she entered.

"Welcome back, Mother!"

Chapter 5

Kin

Village of Loxa, Caledonia

Mid-Summer, 210 AD

Katie had hoped that after a day or two, she might simply wake up back in her own time and place. They had fallen asleep to arrive in ancient Scotland; it stood to reason that the trick was to fall back asleep and go home. It hadn't worked. She had hoped that perhaps if they went back to the battlefield that it might be the solution. It hadn't been possible to try. For one thing, she had to wait for John to recover enough that they could travel together. For another, she wasn't sure how to get there.

Instead, she was trapped as something of a village leader. As weeks went by and John grew stronger, she discovered she wasn't as fully in charge as it had first appeared. There were a number of women who took a key role in managing village affairs. The men, for the most part, hunted and fought with one another. It was a simpler, quieter existence than she was used to and she had a hard time adapting to a rural existence.

Strangest of all in her new life was Lair. The girl was a teen, around the same age as the woman who had died during the battle with the "Africans," or an African contingent of the Roman Army, as she later learned. Pretending she was testing her knowledge, she had decided to get information from the woman she was told was her daughter.

"The Roman soldiers only come from the rest of the island. True or false?" She stated as a quiz question as they spent a quiet evening together. She had come from John's tent earlier, where she was finding that their talks were growing more and more intimate, basic, and connecting. It was hard to put into words, but the tensions from before the time travel had almost completely vanished from the moment the spear had embedded itself into his foot.

Her teenage daughter rolled her eyes, in a move that could easily be recognized from any era in history. "No, they come from all over the empire. You fought soldiers from Africa during your last raid, remember?"

"Of course. But I'm checking to see what you know-"

"I know plenty." She was doodling with a piece of chalky rock on a stone, creating intricately detailed circles as she worked. "You can ask me anything at all about the Romans and I'll know it. I know more than you think, Mother."

"And why do you say that?" She asked, suddenly interested. Katie liked the girl but didn't feel all that strongly connected to her as a mother should. She hadn't brought her up, and she found it extremely difficult to believe that she had a teen daughter. After all, she wasn't even 30 yet, in this time period or in the future. She'd have had to have had this girl when she was 14 or 15 herself, it seemed.

Her daughter pretended not to hear her. Another patented teen move. She shook her head, annoyed.

She thought it might be time to give her a compliment. "By the way, your artwork is amazing. You do this a great deal; I'm impressed."

"I have been practicing a lot." Lair confessed, a proud smile playing about her lips.

"That will help. Do you think you could do something like that for our pottery? I'd love to see you work that in the next time we make pots." She had discovered that her counterpart in this life had done a good deal of pottery. It made sense to her; surely she didn't spend all her time fighting raids and telling people what to do.

"I suppose." Lair had clammed up then, and she'd been unable to get her to say much more after that. It seemed whenever they talked that the girl was hiding something from her, but it was hard to be sure what.

The next day, she took her worries to John. She was spending a lot of time in his tent, she found, more than she might have back in their own time. She'd climb into his bed, a raised palette covered in furs, and run her hands across his chest, looking at his foot and hoping nothing would go wrong. Amazingly, he hadn't suffered any serious infection; Fyfa the healer certainly knew her job.

"I have no doubt she's keeping secrets from you. She's a teen." John suggested. "Did you keep things from your parents at her age?"

"Well, sure. You." She gave him a little kiss on his cheek and he smiled.

"Yeah, but that was different. We were kids. Your daughter is..."

"What?" She wasn't sure why she felt defensive, but an oddly motherly sensation kicked in.

"In this time, you know she's an adult, right? Childhood is incredibly short in the Roman era. I'm surprised she's not married yet."

"Are you kidding?" She felt offended despite the fact she knew he was right.

He held up both his hands. "Hey, don't hurt me. Wounded man here."

She snickered. "You going to use that excuse the entire time we're in Caledonia?"

"Well, only if it'll keep me from playing starter, coach. The other team is kind of brutal."

"I know what you mean." She sighed. "Honestly, we need to find some way to-"

They heard screaming. "What was that?" John asked.

A powerful bolt tore through the tent with the strength and speed of a bullet. It tore a gaping hole only a foot above where they were laying. Had either of them been sitting up, they would have been skewered.

They both leapt to their feet. "What are you doing?" Katie demanded when she saw John grab a sword.

"I'm well enough." He insisted. "Besides, if I don't fight, your word won't protect me from the rest of the clan. I need to earn my keep."

From outside, the source of the problem was clear.

"The Romans are here!"

Chapter 6

Love Rekindled

Village of Loxa, Caledonia

Mid-Summer, 210 AD

When Katie and John exited the tent they could see most of the village was ready for the fight. Beitidh and Caltram were already armed and running towards the source of the attack, rushing in the direction of the tent.

"No!" Katie shouted. The pair stopped in their tracks.

"What would you have us do?" Beitidh asked, annoyed by the delay.

Katie pointed to her left. "Caltram and J- and Nechtan, I mean, you take our best warriors, go behind the Romans, and attack them from that direction. When you have harmed them, run. When they pursue, turn upon them and attack when they aren't expecting it. Draw them away. Beitidh," She turned to her sister. "Take a few warriors and lead our elderly and children just outside of town and prepare to go into the hills if you see we are losing. I will defend the village as long as I can with those who remain. When the Romans become too much for us, we will retreat. We can't win this fight, but we can make them regret this attack." She warned.

Though John looked as though he'd like to question her directions, the others obeyed without a word. A number of Caledonian warriors rallied around Katie and followed her towards the Romans.

She felt her heart race, afraid to face Rome's professional troops. What did she really know about war, anyway? It was a ridiculous idea, the notion that she could face the power of Rome on her own, using her own tactics. She'd never even served in the military in her own time.

She watched a man standing beside her felled by a Roman archer. She'd already learned, by talking with the tacticians among her tribe, that the Romans had a few archers among them. However, it was believed that there weren't as many troops as before. Some had even thought they would give up the Antonine Wall and possibly withdraw many miles to the south. That had been, it seemed, a wrong assessment.

She could see the gleam of their armor as her clan raced across the ground between the soldiers and the village, trying to cover terrain before more arrows could be loosed to fell them. A few of her men fell, but soon they were among the Romans with their axes and short swords. She was amazed to find she could actually wield a sword; apparently whatever skills she'd had in this life carried through.

She knew she needed to kill her enemies, yet, she couldn't bring herself to do it. Instead, she worked very hard to force the soldiers to lose their weapons in the fight, wounding them as a last resort. If forced, she'd injure her opponent to force them out of the battle. She didn't even enjoy doing that. However, the sight of her tribesmen lying dead nearby enraged her. The Romans didn't accept surrender, as she knew. Instead, they'd kill every man in the tribe and enslave the surviving women and children. The battle was one of survival.

As things started to look like they might turn against the Caledonians, they heard the Roman commander call a retreat. Their rear flank had been hit hard, forcing the line she and others were fighting to become thin and vulnerable. The route forced the Romans to flee, something the Caledonians were amazed to see happen.

She was ecstatic when she met John and Caltram, both bloodied but excited. "You should have seen them flee!" John gushed, thrilled by their victory. "They were completely unprepared for your flanking maneuver."

"And Nechtan killed four men!" Caltram announced, his voice booming. "He drove them before him as a whirlwind! Truly impressive."

Before all of the tribe, Katie walked over to John, put her arms around him, and kissed her husband. When they had finished, she announced. "I will take Nechtan as my new husband."

The warriors smiled and slapped them on the back in congratulations. Caltram and Beitidh seemed pleased by the announcement; not that either were too surprised. Everyone in the village had probably seen it coming, but approved of this happy announcement on the field of a victorious battle.

"We have won, but they will be back." Kate warned. "We should go to the place of refuge for a time, the old fort. Gather what animals we will need, strike the tents. We will take everything we can from the village with us into the hills to our fort."

Her people scattered to do as she bid, with the exception of Caltram and Beitidh. Her sister, putting her hands on her hips, gave her a wry smile.

"It seems you were right. This time." She suggested.

"Every time, sis." She countered, then laughed. "Okay, not every time. Most of the time?"

Beitidh shook her head and walked away with Caltram.

Alone at last, John wrapped his arms around his wife. "I'm glad to have this second chance with you. I want you to know I'm going to take it seriously. Trust me; we'll never go back to what it was."

"I know." She said. Touching his face gently, she pressed herself close to him. "This is going to take a few hours. Want to help me pack my things?"

"Absolutely, Mrs. Duncan."

They returned to her hut. Tired, dirty, and cut, they weren't too tired for lovemaking. It was almost as though a desperate mission had arisen within them both as they looked at one another, desire building for the first time since they'd been brought into the forgotten past.

They quickly peeled away their clothing, helping each other become naked, and rushing to be together in her bed. For a time, they simply touched, moving against one another and happy to simply feel human, breathing, enjoying touch. When he entered her, she gasped, rubbing her hands along his sweaty back. As he moved shallow at first, then deeper still inside her, holding her hands in his in the darkness, she arched her back and gasped. Her smile widened as the excitement built, thinking of the battle and the joy at surviving, unharmed by the dangers they'd faced and beaten together. She'd never felt as alive before facing the horror of close, personal combat. She pushed herself against him, urging him to bring her to a hard orgasm.

What she most desired, most wanted, was to feel that there was more to their sex than just momentary joy. Even as they brought each other to their release, she held onto that feeling. As they came, she knew they had found it. They'd found each other again.

"You really want to do this, right? Get married?" She asked after it was over. She knew he did, but she needed to be sure.

"Yes. Absolutely. Will you marry me, Katie? For the first time?"

"It is the first time, isn't it?" She realized with a smile. "Almost two thousand years before the next. Yes, I will. Now and forever."

That night, the couple led the Caledonians away from the village and towards a safer home.

~ Passage Through Time ~

Chapter 7

The Fort

Hills near Loxa, Caledonia

Late Summer, 210 AD

The Caledonian's refuge proved to be a sturdy, if long abandoned fort several miles into the rugged Scottish hills north. After comparing notes, John and Katie guessed that they were around twenty miles from the battle they'd taken part in on their arrival. Others had told them that was around five miles from the Antonine Wall. The Iron Age fort (according to John, and Katie had no reason to doubt him) had proven to be a secure defensive ground for the clan in previous times of serious peril. Though Romans did patrol the vicinity in search of stray villagers over the next week or so, the official policy appeared to be more along the lines of "let bygones be bygones." That was fine with Katie. The less she had to worry about, the better.

One evening, her sister had come to her to let her know that Caltram had finally suggested they marry. She was thrilled for the woman, whom she'd grown close to. With Lair, she prepared her sister a nice meal of venison, leeks and kale. The women sat around the fire together, talking about what married life would be like.

"I know I'm late to it, of course." Beitidh suggested, quietly. She was uncharacteristically shy as the three enjoyed the comforts of the fire. The men had gone off for their own meal and discussion. "But I couldn't see myself with anyone else. He's been very good to me lately, sister."

"Caltram is a good man." Katie agreed. Lair had gone quiet after having eaten half her food and set it aside. Instead, she was messing with a piece of pottery again, drawing on it with the ashy end of a burnt stick. She was drawing the face of a young man, or so it appeared. He looked incredibly lifelike. There was a quality to it that seemed familiar to Katie. She'd seen Lair do many drawings, usually of animals, symbols, and the like. She'd never drawn a person so accurately.

"That's incredible work, Lair." She complimented the girl. Her daughter- she was beginning to think of her as such, strangely- gave a shy smile in response as she did every time she was complimented. "Have you been practicing while you're on your own during the evening?"

Lair had taken to wandering on the hills by herself, despite the dangers of the soldiers. She was of an age she was certainly allowed, so long as she got all of her work done for the day, though Katie was very worried about her being away from the safety of the fort. She'd come back breathless and happy from each trip. Katie assumed a guy might be involved, but didn't pry. It wasn't entirely her business, anyway; if she asked permission to marry, she supposed she'd have to give it, as was custom of the clan.

"I have. Some." Lair turned quickly to Beitidh. "You are so lucky, Aunt! I hope I will marry an honorable warrior one day. Someone tall, handsome, strong- a protector and a friend. You have all of that in Caltram."

Her Aunt laughed brightly. "I suppose I have! I don't know why we were so shy for so long about proclaiming our intentions. It always seemed the timing was wrong. But now we are committed to it. I think... I think it may have been seeing how you and Nechtan found love."

"How so?" Katie asked, surprised.

"The whole clan has been inspired by you both. To be truthful, neither of you seemed very... well, that is that no one had ever suspected you two were interested in one another before the battle near the Roman's wall. You were hardly friendly. No one saw him as a good warrior either. But you were right! Your prophecy was truthful and now I can hardly imagine our people without you both leading the way. You in particular, of course, Kate." She quickly demurred.

"You are kind, sister." Lair excused herself and left their fire to go outside. When she was sure they were alone, the sisters shared secretive grins with one another.

"Do you think she's off to find her lover?" Beitidh suggested, keeping her voice down.

"Do I think so? I know it. That girl is seeing someone. But for the life of me, I can't tell who it is. None of the men of the tribe have given even a little hint of their interest."

A playful smile crossed Beitidh's face. "Want to find out who?"

"How?"

"Let's follow her. She can't have gone far."

"Oh, yes! This might be fun. But listen, we must absolutely not interfere or bother them. I would feel terrible, you understand?"

"Yes, yes." Beitidh said dismissively. They put out their fire and barely spotted the back of the girl's back as she made her way through the quiet, night-time fort.

They were surprised to see she was leaving through the front entrance. "Very secretive." Katie whispered to her sister as they crouched behind a cart near the entrance.

"Well, of course, silly. If you don't want the whole village to talk you need to go somewhere, you know, private." Beitidh replied.

The two stole out into the darkness, stalking their relative as silently as they knew how. Katie had been given many opportunities to practice her quiet movements on short raids against the Romans, so she tried to put her skills to good use.

A short distance from the fort and beyond a creek crossing, they spied her entering a cave. "Should we draw nearer? I don't know what we can see." Beitidh asked.

"I'll do it. Wait here." Katie covered a giggle and crept up on the cave.

She got as far as the entrance, where she could see a soft light. "No, you're looking at it all wrong." A young man said within the cave, his low baritone a smooth, accented tongue to Katie's ears. Her breath caught. Lair was seeing a foreigner? That was certainly strange. Where would she have met one?

She slowly, carefully inched her way around the edge of the cave entrance so she could see without being seen. Lair was standing before the rock face cavern wall, painting a mural. A young man was sitting beside her, painting on a piece of what she took to be paper. The two were close and exchanging long, loving glances with one another.

By his appearance, manner, and dress, it was at once obvious what she was seeing. The man was clearly one of the African Roman garrison members.

Chapter 8

The Cave

Hills near Loxa, Caledonia

Early Fall, 210 AD

"What the hell is going on here?"

Katie hadn't meant to shout her words, but the sight of the clan's bitter enemy with her daughter drove her to it. She stepped directly into the entrance, shocked by what she was seeing.

The two immediately stopped what they were doing. Lair drew close to the soldier, who stood and put a protective arm around her. "Who are- oh no!" He said, recognizing her.

Katie wished she had her sword with her, but knowing Beitidh did, she nearly called for her to come. Before she could do anything, Lair cried out, "Wait!"

"Wait? For what? How long have you been meeting with a man who helped kill your own kin, Lair?" Lair didn't answer, so she repeated it. "How long?"

"This summer. You never cared where I went! Septimus is good to me. I love him."

Katie kept her hands firmly planted on her hips. "Come away from him, Lair. Now."

"Why? Because he is an outsider?" Lair had a defiant look on her face she'd never seen before.

"What? No, I'd never- Lair, he's a Roman soldier. Think about it, won't you?"

"Yes, he's a soldier, mother, but that's not where his heart lies. Tell her."

The young man, intimidated by Katie's fearsome reputation, spoke in a quiet tone. "I was an artist in my homeland. The Romans came, we fought them, but they made me a slave. I went to Rome and served an artist. He allowed me to paint, to learn their ways of making a face more realistic. He was very old and died, but his family moved to Volubilis and took me with them. This is a city in Africa."

Beitidh was approaching, but Kate sensed her presence would make things worse; she was armed, as she almost always was, with her short sword and might run the young man through on sight. She motioned for her sister to stay away while he continued talking. "Go on."

"In this city, many people were recruited into the legion. I escaped my masters and became a soldier. But my heart has never been in killing. When we were sent here, I am ashamed to say I deserted. But you must understand that I had discovered in my first fight that I don't have the heart of a killer. I see your tribe as deserving of your own ways, customs, and lives, much as I had back in my own home country. I don't want to kill. I want to paint.

"Come see what we've been working on." Lair implored her mother.

"In a moment." Kate went back to Beitidh, who looked quite nervous.

"Well?" Her sister demanded.

"He's... he's an outcast." Katie said, leaving it at that. "Tell no one. Go back and wait for me to speak with you more."

"Very well."

Katie returned to the cave and walked over to the wall painting. She was momentarily taken aback, then slowly began to smile.

On the wall was a mostly finished painting of John and Katie. It was a precise replica of the illustration she'd seen in the book back in Glasgow.

On the paper nearby, Septimus was copying Lair's work down on a piece of paper. His work was very good and much closer to the illustration she'd seen, but the wall was the masterpiece.

"When will you be done?" Katie asked.

"I'm not sure. By the end of harvest?" Lair suggested. "It's silly, I know. I hope I haven't offended you, mother."

Katie gently placed her hand on her daughter's shoulder. "Offended? Impossible. I'm honored and proud of you." She gave her daughter a light kiss on the forehead.

She looked over at the soldier. "You know the wall better than anyone I've met. Could you take me back that way if I asked?"

He looked concerned, then nodded his head in agreement. "I could do that. Why would you wish this?"

She didn't tell him that it was to find the place she and John had come into their time from, but had a better excuse at the ready. "There is a rumor that the wall will be abandoned soon. I'd like to confirm it. We will meet again when harvest comes and the painting is complete. You will take Nechtan and I there at that time."

"As you wish." He affirmed.

She wasn't sure why the completion of the painting was essential, but given they had been looking at it when they'd been transported, it made a certain kind of sense to Katie. At least- she hoped so.

Chapter 9

Samhain

Approaching the Antonine Wall

Late Fall, 210 AD

The harvest was a decent one, despite the poor conditions of the terrain, and the animals would get the tribe through the winter. It was time to go, if it were possible, as the Samhain festival drew near.

It had been hard giving her sister what she thought might be her last hug. She'd used the excuse that she had to finish some pottery that day after having spent much of the morning in the company of Beitidh and Caltram. But as she turned away, tears had fallen without note and in secret. Beitidh had called out, hopefully, "I'll see you this evening for supper?"

"We'll see." She'd replied. There was an even harder parting drawing near, and she wasn't looking forward to it.

John was ready near the gate, as they'd discussed. It was late in the afternoon, with plenty of daylight left for them to begin their effort. He looked hopeful. "Shall we do some hunting?" He suggested, mostly for the benefit of anyone who'd overhear.

"It's a good day for it." She'd responded breezily enough. But as they left behind the fort, she couldn't help but look back, sad to see the village she'd led now about to disappear from her life. She wondered what would become of it.

The pair found the cave and there, Lair and Septimus were putting the final touches on their work. Katie hadn't wanted to risk anything happening to the artists, and so hadn't taken John to see the cave. She'd feared they might be followed or seen going in that direction, and Lair was taking enough risk to go to him as often as she did. Of course, he'd known about what was being done and agreed that her idea regarding seeing the illustration completed was a sound one.

When John saw their faces and bodies perfectly recreated on the wall, he was stunned. "My God." He muttered. "It is something beautiful. Lair, I'm impressed."

The teen really did blush at this. "Septimus has taught me much." She explained.

"Regardless, I can't believe I'm seeing this. Are you done?"

Lair took a hard look over her work. "Yes. Finished now."

"Then it is the perfect time to head to the wall. Septimus, you'll lead the way."

"Of course." The man said, setting his own paper aside to dry. "If you are ready, I am. But we must be cautious."

"That, I think, is something we can manage." Katie replied.

***

The four people managed to draw quite close to the battlegrounds. The bodies had long ago been taken from the field, but to Katie it seemed they were still there. She didn't understand how she could still retain her modern aversion to the sights of war, yet be able to draw from a more primitive, stronger instinct to fight at the same time. She wondered if she stayed there much longer if the old Katie would lose out and disappear.

She didn't plan to stick around and find out.

"This was the place, wasn't it, John?"

He nodded. "The exact same. You were there. I was roughly... here?"

"John? What are you talking about?" Lair asked them both with bewilderment.

Kate went to her daughter, put her arms around the girl, and hugged her close. She kissed her cheek. "Be careful and be happy with Septimus. I will always love you, okay?"

The girl looked deeply confused. But as Katie stepped closer to where she thought she'd been, she felt a sudden tiredness overtaking her. "This is it, John." She said. "Goodbye to you both. Take care of each other."

She had a moment to see the confusion and fear on both young people's faces before the ground started to spin up towards her.

***

Glasgow, Scotland

June 15, 2015

"Ah! I've found the book." Professor Wellesley shouted. Katie snapped her head up from the table, her head spinning as she did so. All the lights were on.

John also looked shocked and rudely awakened. "Katie?" He murmured. "Katie!" His face was lit by excitement and joy.

She fell into his arms and the old man was shocked to see the two passionately embracing against the old wooden table.

"I say!" He muttered. Then more quietly as he tottered off to another aisle to give them a moment's peace, taking to talking to himself. "True bibliophiles those two. Can't say the wife ever gave me that response to books but... could try I suppose. What could it hurt?"

***

They'd had to stay on another week to find it, but it was worth it. The Duncans, wearing backpacks and having already been out in the woods for a few days already, climbed the short hike past the little creek and towards the cave. They'd left the ruins of the Iron Age fort behind once they'd found it. Out of an abundance of caution, they'd agreed not to retrace their steps to the sight of the battle, but they had visited the site of the original village. Disappointingly, it had been a farmer's field. It in no way resembled what they recalled to be the little Caledonian village of Loxa.

The cave, though, was a welcome sight. They hurried to the entrance, eager to see what was left to be seen.

John flicked on a flashlight as they entered, letting the light play out across the wall. They were there, all right. Much of their bodies had peeled away and been wrecked by time and wear. But Katie's face and head were very clearly visible, if deeply faded. John was almost entirely visible as well, with an ear and part of his head missing and chipped off. But there was no denying it; Lair's work had somehow survived the ages.

Katie drew her man in close to her. "I can feel them here still. Lair, Septimus, Beitidh, and Caltram. Do you?"

"Of course, my warrior princess." He said. Before their lips met, he added, "They're here and will be inside us always."

***

About the Author

From Scotland to Egypt, South America to Japan - travel the world in romance. William Newell enjoys creating imaginative novellas which are captivating. Come home each evening and explore a deep relationship between animated characters while learning the history of a new part of the world.

William is passionate about creating deep connections between the characters in his works to bring them alive off the page, while adding a modern twist to their everyday obstacles. Expect humor and whit while living the adventure in the richly detailed canvas of these stories.

His goal is to enrich and entertain, providing an avenue of enjoyment which sparks the creativity and imagination of his readers. Besides writing, William's passion is learning about the history of the world's most unique cultures. He aims to weave his own knowledge into each individual story he creates.

Visit William Newell's Author Page on Amazon

Preview of the next book in the series...

"Return To Scotland"

Chapter 1

Return to Caledonia

Glasgow Airport, Glasgow, Scotland

June 29, 2018

Even as the plane touched down on the tarmac of Glasgow Airport, Katie Duncan couldn't believe they were coming back. Though an American, she couldn't help but think of Scotland as home. There were good reasons for her feelings as she watched thick ropes of rain streak across her tiny window view of Scotland. They weren't reasons she could share with her family back in Chicago, of course. But there were reasons.

"Are you okay?" Her husband John asked, lightly touching her cheek with his fingertips. What a difference in closeness there was between them three years after their last trip. Their first visit to Scotland had been marked by tension, the kind a couple experiences only weeks or months before one of them contacts a lawyer. But of course, by the time they'd left Britain, all of that had changed.

"Yes. No. I'm sorry, I don't really know what to feel. How do you feel?" The plane was taxiing down the runway and soon their fellow flyers would be hustling to grab bags from overhead compartments. She and John knew they'd remain seated for a while. They needed time to process that they'd returned.

"It's different for me. I didn't leave a sister and a daughter behind. That life we left really was someone else's for me."

"I suppose that's true." She murmured. She knew what she was feeling; competing urges to run back to the place where it had all begun, a little medieval museum in Glasgow. That part of her felt that perhaps she could once again be transported in time to Roman-occupied Scotland. The other part of her wanted nothing more than to buy a ticket back for Chicago and run away from those feelings.

In 2015, the year before she'd turned 30, she and John had both been transported back to a time when the Caledonian people were the Scots, and everyone to the south of them were Romans. There was no scientific or sensible explanation for what had happened to them, and they had decided against trying sharing their experiences with anyone once they'd gotten back. It was too insane to be believed, and they hadn't wanted to be treated like kooks. Yet, it had happened. They'd spent an entire summer leading a small Caledonian tribe where Katie had been mother to a teen daughter. The daughter had created an astonishingly lifelike portrait of John and Katie in a cave not far from Glasgow. This was their only reminder and proof of their experience once they'd managed to return back home.

An overwhelming desire to see the cave once more had driven them both back. That, and a pull that Katie couldn't quite explain even to herself. It was as if Scotland wanted them to come back and she were powerless to resist, like salmon returning instinctually from where they'd spawned. She didn't try to interpret her feelings to John, and when she'd proposed the return trip he'd been quick enough to agree to the idea- too quick, as though he were on the brink of making the exact same proposal. She suspected he felt the same instinct, but that he didn't feel any more comfortable putting it into words than she did.

As the other passengers hustled by their seat, John quietly held her hand as she continued to look into the grey sky. "If you could go there again... see them again... would you want to?"

She took a deep breath and let it out. "No. But I do want to write about it. I didn't tell you honey, but that's what I plan to do."

"Like... fiction?"

"No. Non-fiction. I'm going to tell the truth."

It was his turn to sigh, but when he breathed into her long, curly red hair she could tell his sigh wasn't the same as her surrender. His was one of released tension. "I was afraid you'd say that."

She turned and looked him in the eye, holding his gaze a long moment before speaking. "I have to do this."

"I know." He nodded. "You understand that it may be hard to publish? That if your boss finds out, you could lose your job?"

Katie was a reporter back home, a job she enjoyed and rarely took breaks from. She'd learned to schedule more time away so she and John were together, and for his part, he made sure he wasn't as wrapped up in his projects and hobbies as before. During the day he was a computer programmer and on weekends he still studied history, wrote music, and took photographs. These days, all three of his hobbies had found room for Katie, whereas in the bad old days the two had kept as far apart as possible for those interests. He still made time just for himself and for his friends, yet he and Katie always seemed to find an excuse to spend time together as well.

"It'll still be worth it. I'll find another job if I absolutely have to."

He kissed her, gently and sweetly. She no longer felt the familiar tickle of his dark beard, as he'd shaved it off just before the trip. She kind of missed it, but didn't miss how it could be scratchy at times. "I support you, you know that."

"Yeah. I do." She beamed in response.

The plane had nearly emptied out, so they gathered their things and went to the front of the plane. "Welcome to Glasgow, folks." The chipper stewardess suggested as they disembarked. "Stay as long as you please."

The Duncans exchanged a glance and nearly laughed. "Oh, we love it here. You could say we and Scotland go way back." John replied, and when he did, Katie covered an actual laugh, pretending it was a sneeze.

***

A Cave in Western Scotland

June 29, 2018

The wall was every bit the same as they expected. Unvisited, untouched and unknown by anyone in hundreds of years. It helped that the entrance was completely covered with vegetation, so well hidden that you had to know what you were looking for to find it.

Katie held up a flashlight and let it illuminate the work her long-dead daughter had created on the wall. In the foreground was Katie herself; her high cheekbones and red hair were unmistakable. The style may have been Roman-influenced thanks to the teen daughter's Roman artist boyfriend, but there was also a flair that was unmistakably the young woman's. To her right and slightly in the background was John's face, more weather-worn than Katie's; he was most noticeably missing an ear. Both of them had lost most of their bodies, and the whimsical background that had framed them both was mostly faded and lost to history.

John took many pictures, as they'd agreed. "You should write about how you feel being here."

"I will." She agreed.

"No. Now. While the thoughts are fresh."

"Oh! Good idea." She pulled out a small computer pad and began to type away.

After a time, she seemed to have captured all of the disparate thoughts and emotions that had been dredged up by revisiting the cave. John sat beside her and she rested her head on his shoulder, wiping away a few tears. "That's all I can do for now."

"Sure. It's going to take a lot out of you doing this, you know."

"I know."

He kissed the top of her head. "So, you're just going to write about the Caledonians, is that the idea?"

"If I'm going to write this properly," she mused, "I need to document my family. Not just the Caledonians. We Cathcarts, just like your Duncan family, came from Scotland. It's going to take some research, but I need to find out what happened to the other Scots in my family.

"Makes sense. So... where to now?" He asked.

"Cathcart, dear."

He looked confused, so she explained. "It's part of Glasgow, but it was once its own town."

He nodded and they stood up. "Long hike back into town. Where will we start?"

She smiled. "Where does every American searching for their roots start? We'll visit a genealogist."

***

Grab your copy of "Return to Scotland" on Amazon

A Note From The Author

"If you enjoyed this book and found it entertaining, I welcome you to leave an honest review. It not only helps me understand the pros and cons of my work but can provide value to others considering giving this story a shot! I will take all reviews very seriously and would like to thank you for your time reading this story, regardless. Thank you again for your purchase and be on the lookout for others by William Newell."

Made in the USA
Monee, IL
11 May 2021

68403780R00059